NOW, PRINCESS ADRIENNE, WITH MY SUPERIOR MASTERY OF THE SWORD I SHALL PUT AN END TO YOUR QUEST.

THE THING IN THE DUNGEON

ILLUSTRATED by NANCY KING

NOT SO FAST, CAD!

OUCH!

DON'T UNDER-ESTIMATE PRINCESS ADRIENNE!

DON'T YOU KNOW? GIRLS KICK BUTT!

YOU PLAY TOO ROUGH, ADRIENNE.

I DON'T THINK WE SHOULD BE HERE.

STOP WORRYING AND CHECK OUT WHAT'S IN THE DUNGEON!

WHAT'S A DRAGON DOING IN OUR DUNGEON?

WHO CARES? LOOK HOW AWESOME IT IS!

AWESOME? IT'S A...

SHHH! SOMEONE'S COMING!

I ASK FOR A GUARDIAN FOR ALIZE AND THIS IS WHAT THEY BRING ME.

PERHAPS IF WE RAISE ONE FROM A HATCHLING IT'LL BE A SUITABLE GUARDIAN.

DARLING, THIS THING IS MUCH TOO VICIOUS. IT'LL EAT OUR DAUGHTER ALIVE.

I'M STILL NOT SURE WE'RE DOING THE RIGHT THING.

NO, THIS IS HOW IT HAS TO BE.

I'LL HAVE THEM FIND SOMETHING SMARTER, BUT NO LESS DANGEROUS.

WE NEED A REAL MAN FOR AN HEIR.

IT'S FOR THE GOOD OF THE KINGDOM, MY LOVE.

I SUPPOSE...

GET OFF OF ME!

SHHH!

THE MERRY ADVENTURES OF YOUNG PRINCE

ASH

ILLUSTRATED by QUINNE LARSEN

SO, I'D JUST BEEN CROWNED CHAMPION OF THE WESTLAND TOURNAMENT AND I WAS THANKING THE COURT FOR HAVING ME.

THE TIME I WRESTLED A TROLL?

THAT TALE MAY BE A BIT BAWDY FOR THE EARS OF YOUNG MAIDS.

PERHAPS WE SHOULD FIND A VENUE A BIT MORE...PRIVATE.

TEE HEE!

WHEN THAT VULGAR PRINCE VALMAR SLANDERED THE NAME OF ONE OF THE COURTLY LADIES.

HOW DARE YOU SWAGGER AROUND HERE LIKE A PEACOCK, LITTLE PRINCE.

YOU KNOW AS WELL AS I DO THAT WILMAUT THREW THAT MATCH.

AND WHY WOULD WILMAUT DO THAT AFTER HE BEAT YOU SO SOUNDLY?

BECAUSE LIKE SO MANY OF THESE FOOLS, HE'S AFRAID TO LAY A HAND ON THE HIGH PRINCE OF ASHLAND.

YOU'RE JUST LUCKY IT WASN'T ME YOU FOUGHT.

NATURALLY, I HAD TO REPRIMAND THE MAN.

WELL VALMAR, AS YOU'VE ALREADY BEEN BEATEN TO A PULP ONCE TODAY...

...HOW ABOUT A DIFFERENT KIND OF CHALLENGE.

WHAT?

THE BLACK FOREST.

IT'S THE BORDER BETWEEN MY REALM AND YOURS.

IT'S SWARMING WITH HOSTILE ELVES AND WOLVES AND TOO DENSE TO RIDE A HORSE ANYWHERE BUT THE ROAD.

AND?

I'LL RACE YOU TO THE OTHER SIDE, ON FOOT. THE FIRST ONE TO REACH ASHLAND TAKES THE TITLE FOR THIS TOURNAMENT.

YOU'RE A *MADMAN*, ASH. IF THE WOLVES DON'T HAVE YOU FOR DINNER THE ELVES WILL LEAVE YOU HANGING FROM *A TREE*.

IT'S STARTING TO SOUND LIKE YOU'RE AFRAID.

WHAT DO YOU THINK, LADIES?

IS THE GREAT PRINCE VALMAR A COWARD?

TEE HEE!

ALRIGHT, YOU'RE ON. BUT NONE OF YOUR CUTE LITTLE TRICKS!

WHEN DO YOU PROPOSE THIS RACE START?

NOW!

ASH! GET BACK HERE!

PIN-UP BY TRESSA BOWLING

TO BE CONTINUED...

I'M NOT RUNNING AWAY FROM YOU.

WHAT DID YOU SAY?

HUH?

YOU SAID SOMETHING.

OH, I SAID I'M GLAD I RAN AWAY WITH YOU.

THE SMITHS

ILLUSTRATED by JULES RIVERA

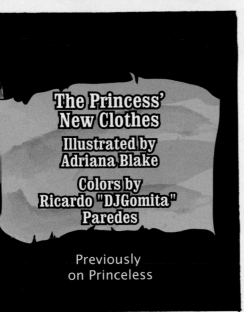

The Princess' New Clothes

Illustrated by
Adriana Blake

Colors by
Ricardo "DJGomita"
Paredes

Previously
on Princeless

WHAT ARE YOU DOING TO MY TOWER?

Adrienne Ashe
Angelica's Younger Sister

ANGELICA JUST DOESN'T UNDERSTAND THERE'S MORE TO LIFE THAN *SITTING AROUND BEING PRETTY.*

I'VE ALWAYS BEEN CONVINCED I WASN'T *PRETTY* ENOUGH.

Café Angelica

I THOUGHT MAYBE, INSTEAD OF MAKING ALL THESE THINGS FOR *ME*, THE CAMP COULD MAYBE MAKE SOME THINGS TO HELP PEOPLE WHO *NEED* IT.

YOU KNOW, *POOR* AND *UGLY* ONES.

I STAYED UP ALL NIGHT TO GET THAT DRESS FINISHED.

BUT I FINISHED IT. SURE, IT WASN'T AS EASY AS I THOUGHT BUT I *FINISHED* IT.

I'D ALWAYS *DREAMED* OF BEING A MODEL. NOW ANGELICA WAS FINALLY GIVING ME THAT *CHANCE*.

I COULDN'T *WAIT* TO SEE MY DRESS ON THE RUNWAY.

WELL, WHEN THE PRINCESS' DRESS CAME OUT, EVERYBODY WAS *AWESTRUCK*.

The Merry Adventures
of Prince Ashe
- Episode 2: The Girl -
Illustrated by Jessi Sheron

WHAT KIND OF GIRL DO YOU THINK I AM? OF COURSE I'M **NOT** GOING TO KISS YOU. I JUST **MET** YOU.

WHAT? I CAN'T! WHO?!

GAH!

THERE HE IS!

WHO? ME?

YOU, SON! *YOU*, OF COURSE!

YOUR WINNER!

WINNER?

THE BET, BOY. THE BET.

HIGH PRINCE ASH! TOURNAMENT CHAMPION AND HERO OF THE BLACK FOREST!

HE'S GOING TO BE A GREAT LEADER SOON. I COULD SEE IT IN HIM.

HE'LL BE A GOOD LEADER. HE'S VERY KIND.

SOMETIMES, GREAT LEADERS FORGET THINGS LIKE KINDNESS.

I'M SURE HE'LL FORGET A GREAT *MANY* THINGS WHEN HE BECOMES KING.

HE'LL NEED SOMEONE TO *REMIND* HIM.

NO, I'M AFRAID NOT... SO YOU'LL HAVE TO BE SOMETHING *ELSE*.

YES, BUT NOT A PEASANT GIRL.

Nightlight

Illustrated by Isabelle Melançon

I AM *ANGOISSE ASHE*, THE MIDDLEST SISTER IN A FAMILY *FULL* OF SPECTACULAR PRINCESSES.

I'VE BEEN TRAPPED IN THIS TOWER FOR *FOUR YEARS* NOW. *NO ONE* HAS COME TO RESCUE ME.

mope.

mope.

mope.

NOT THAT I THOUGHT THEY WOULD. WHY *SHOULD* THEY? THERE'S *NOTHING* SPECIAL ABOUT ME.

mope.
mope.

mope.

ALL OF MY OTHER SISTERS ARE PROBABLY *RESCUED* AND *MARRIED OFF* BY NOW.

NOT THAT THEY INVITED *ME* TO ANY OF THE WEDDINGS. WHY WOULD THEY?

HELLO?

HELLO, ANGOISSE.

YOU MUST BE *LOST*.

I ASSURE YOU I AM *NOT*. I AM LOOKING FOR THE HONEY SKINNED MAIDEN THEY CALL ANGOISSE.

DOES IT NOT *CONCERN* YOU THAT I DO NOT APPEAR IN YOUR MIRROR.

WELL, I KINDA FIGUR[E] WHATEVER GUY IS HERE FOR M[E] IS PROBABLY *HIDEOUS* ANYWAY.

I BEG OF YOU, TURN YOUR FACE TOWARD ME SO I MIGHT BASK IN ITS *RADIANCE*.

WHATEVER. YOU'RE IN FOR A BIG *LET DOWN*.

UH...HELLO.

SPEAK AGAIN, SWEET ANGOISSE. YOUR VOICE *NURTURES* MY SOUL, SO LONG IN THE DARK.

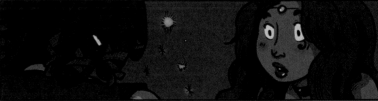

WOW...

REEEEEALLY?

I'VE FLOWN ON NIGHT AIR AS COOL AND CRISP AS A CHILD'S LAUGHTER IN HOPES THAT MY EYES MIGHT HAVE THE BLESSING OF MEETING YOURS TONIGHT.

REALLY, HOW FAR DID YOU COME?

I KNOW NOT THE DISTANCE, FOR INCHES SEEMED MILES KNOWING THAT YOU WERE AT THE OTHER END. I COULD NOT MOVE MY FEET AS QUICKLY AS MY *HEART*.

WOW...

AMAZING... PLEASE TELL ME MORE!

I CAN HEAR THE FLUTTERING OF YOUR HEART LIKE THE WINGS OF THE MOST BEAUTIFUL BUTTERFLY. I FEEL THE WARMTH OF YOUR BODY CALLING TO ME.

WHEN I STAND SO CLOSE TO YOU, I SMELL YOUR SKIN LIKE NIGHTSHADE AND JASMINE.

AND I LONG TO TASTE...

ACTUALLY, I COULD GO FOR A *SANDWICH*. BELOVED, MIGHT I HAVE A HAM AND SWISS?

A-A *SANDWICH*? AREN'T YOU EVEN GOING TO TELL ME YOUR NAME?

RAFAEL, BUT I WOULD *CHANGE* IT IF IT WOULD PLEASE YOU. NOW ABOUT THAT *HAM*...

A WEEK LATER...

SHUFFLE

...RAPHAEL CAME TO SEE ME AGAIN WHILE I SLEPT.

HUH? WHAT'S GOING ON?

I LIKE TO **WATCH** YOU WHEN YOU SLEEP.

UMMM...OKAY, **WHY**?

YOU'RE SO **BEAUTIFUL** WHEN YOU SLEEP. SO **FRAGILE**. I FEEL LIKE I COULD **BREAK** YOU WITH A TOUCH OF MY HAND.

I WANT TO KISS YOU NOW.

THEN WHY DON'T YOU **RESCUE** ME? TAKE ME BACK TO MY FATHER AND WE CAN BE TOGETHER?

ALAS, IT IS THE **KING** WHO KEEPS US APART! IN ORDER FOR US TO BE TOGETHER, I MUST COMPLETE A **QUEST**.

A QUEST? YOU'RE GOING ON A QUEST FOR **ME**?

INDEED MY DARK FLOWER, BUT I THINK IF I WAIT UNTIL THE QUEST IS COMPLETE TO KISS YOU, MY HEART WILL SHRIVEL AND BLOW AWAY.

STILL THOUGH, I'D REALLY LIKE TO **WAIT**.

THE NEXT MORNING.

MISS?

MUHHH??

WHERE--?

YOU'RE IN GRIMMORIUM SWAMP, MISS.

THIS IS *NO* PLACE FOR A YOUNG LADY.

NOW, I REMEMBER. IT WAS THE WORST NIGHT OF MY LIFE! I JUST WANT TO GO BACK TO MY CASTLE...

I PASSED A BIG CASTLE ON THE WAY HERE. IS THAT WHERE YOU'RE FROM?

ARE YOU *PRINCESS ANGOISSE?*

YES. YOU DIDN'T RECOGNIZE ME BEFORE? THEN WHY DID YOU *HELP* ME?

IT SEEMED LIKE THE RIGHT THING TO DO FOR A LADY.

♪ My loooove... I am calling to yoOOOOOu... ♪

LISTEN, OUT HERE IN THE SWAMP YOU CAN'T BE TOO *BUSY*. DO YOU THINK MAYBE I COULD--

MY DAAAARLING!

WHO'S *THIS* GUY?

MY EX-BOYFRIEND!

MY PURPLE ROSE, YOUR WORDS WOUND ME. SAY NOT EX-BOYFRIEND, FOR I HAVE *RETURNED* TO PUT RIGHT MY WRONGS.

YOU *LEFT* ME IN THE SWAMP IN THE MIDDLE OF THE NIGHT!

WHY SHOULD I COME BACK AFTER HOW *MEAN* YOU WERE?

YOU MISTAKE MY *PASSION* FOR MEANNESS! I HAVEN'T STOPPED *CRYING* SINCE I LEFT YOU.

YOU *CRIED* OVER ME?

I WEPT *RIVERS* THAT FLOWED FORTH TO FORM SALTY LAKES OF SADNESS!

SLPOO

ALL RIGHTY THEN. HMMMM...YEAH. ...WELL, I'LL BE GOING NOW.

I *LOVE* YOU.

I LOVE YOU MORE!

TOO MUCH DRAMA...
...THEY DESERVE EACH OTHER MUMBLE, MUMBLE...

I DON'T KNOW. SOMETHING STILL LOOKS *OFF* ABOUT IT.

REALLY? LIKE WHAT?

The Girl with the Giveaway Ears

Illustrated by Tara Abbamondi

IS IT THE VEST? IT'S A LITTLE SMALL FOR ME.

WELL, SINCE WE'RE TRYING NOT TO GET NOTICED, THAT *PLAID* MIGHT BE A BIT MUCH.

ARE YOU KIDDING? THESE PANTS ARE *AWESOME!*

MAYBE WE COULD GET SOME *SHOES* TOO?

NO NO NO NO NO! YOU WON'T GET ME IN SHOES!

I DON'T CARE *WHAT* KIND OF TORTURE YOU THREATEN ME WITH!

WELL, OKAY, THEN. THAT'S A NO ON SHOES.

IF THAT'S EVERYTHING, GO ON OUT AND PAY THE MAN.

UMMM... PAY WITH *WHAT?*

A-HEM.

HEY, BUDDY!

SO, IS *THAT* WHAT THE REAL PRINCE WILCOME IS LIKE? WHEN HE'S NOT LOCKED IN A DUNGEON?

OH NO, THE *REAL* PRINCE WILCOME IS MUCH MORE *POWERFUL* THAN THAT. I WOULD HAVE HAD HIM *HAULED OFF TO THE JAIL* WITHOUT A SECOND THOUGHT.

OH.

I'M STARVING. ARE YOU HUNGRY?

SO, YOU'VE DONE THIS BEFORE?

SIT BACK AND WATCH A *PRO* AT WORK.

CAN I HELP YOU FIND SOMETHING?

DO YOU HAVE ANY DRAGON BERRIES?

DRAGON BERRIES! HA! YOU CAUGHT ME ABOUT THIRTY YEARS TOO LATE. I'M NOT FOOL ENOUGH TO HUNT THOSE ANYMORE. EVER SINCE MY KNEE...

WOW, YOU *HUNTED* THEM YOURSELF?

YOU MUST BE *BRAVE.* DID YOU EVER RUN INTO A *DRAGON?*

THE BIGGEST, MEANEST, COLDEST ICE DRAGON YOU EVER SEEN. EVERYTHING HIS BREATH TOUCHED FROZE INSTANTLY.

WOW!

YOU MUST BE *REALLY* BRAVE.

OH, I WAS ONCE. YOU'RE A SWEET GIRL.

AWW, THANKS. WELL, I'VE GOT TO BE GOING.

CRUNCH

OOF!

SORRY 'BOUT THAT, MA'AM.

OH NO, IT'S ALL RIGHT. I'M FINE.

YOU *DROPPED* SOMETHING...

...YOUNG LADY...

ELF!

EEP!

GET BACK HERE!

WILCOME! HELP ME, PLEASE!

STOP IN THE NAME OF THE KING!

WELL, IT WOULD CERTAINLY BE *EASIER* TO GET OUT OF TOWN WITHOUT A GIANT, GANGLY *ELF GIRL* IN TOW.

STOP THAT ELF!

OH, THIS *STINKS* SO MUCH!

HA! NOW I'VE GOT THEM BEAT.

OOPH!

THAT KEEPS HAPPENING! IT REALLY HURTS!

IT'S ABOUT TO *HURT* MORE, ELF SCUM!

UMMM... THIS IS ALL A MISUNDERSTANDING!

NO MISUNDERSTANDING. ELVES ARE AN INFESTATION.

AND *I'M* THE EXTERMINATOR!

!

NOW THAT YOU'VE ENJOYED THE *FRUIT* OF MY LABORS, ARE YOU READY TO GO?

OOOH! *PUNS!*

HAVE YOU HEARD FROM ANY OF THE OTHER KNIGHTS YET?

Waiting
Illustrated by Jen Vaughn

NAH. EXPECT THEY HAVEN'T DONE ANY BETTER FINDING HIM THAT *WE* HAVE.

GENTLEMEN, WELCOME TO LION'S REST.

MY NAME IS AISHA AND I'LL BE SERVING--

--YOU'RE *WHO* NOW?

MY NAME IS *AISHA*.

THAT'S *NOT* A GRASSLANDS NAME.

APOLOGIES, MISS AISHA. SIR ROCKS IS A BIT GRUFF. WHAT HE MEANT TO SAY IS, YOU HAVE A *BEAUTIFUL* NAME. WHERE IS IT FROM?

UM...MY FAMILY IS FROM THE SOUTHERN DESERT.

LOVELY PLACE. MY PARTNER AND I ARE BOUNTY HUNTERS, SO WE NOTICE WHEN THINGS ARE *OUT OF PLACE*.

IF YOU DON'T MIND MY SAYING SO, YOU'RE TOO *LOVELY* FOR THIS PLACE.

OOOKAY. WHAT WOULD YOU GENTLEMEN LIKE?

GROG.

A COMPLICATED QUESTION, MISS AISHA, BUT I'LL HAVE WHATEVER YOU RECOMMEND.

WELL...

JUST *SURPRISE* ME, DARLING.

IF YOU SAY SO.

ONE MORE THING, MISS AISHA. WAITRESSES SE A LOT OF PEOPLE. DOE *THIS MAN* LOOK FAMILIAR?

I'M SORRY, BUT NO.

OH, MY *GOSH*, EESHA. WHAT ARE THEY *LIKE*?

I AM SO *CREEPED OUT* RIGHT NOW!

THE LITTLE ONE IS JUST RUDE AND I THINK THE TALL ONE IS *HITTING ON* ME. HE *TOUCHED* MY HAND!

HITTING ON YOU? OH, GOSH! HE'S SO *CUTE*. I BET THEY'RE *KNIGHTS*.

ONE OF THEM CALLED THE OTHER ONE "SIR" SOMETHING.

I JUST WANT THEM OUT BEFORE THEY GET ANY *CREEPIER*.

YOU'RE SO WEIRD AISHA. DON'T YOU WANT A KNIGHT TO WHISK YOU AWAY FROM HERE?

UGH. I WANT TO GET *OUT* OF HERE, BUT GODDESS FORBID.

THERE'S A *SECRET EXIT* IN THE BACK!

THIS WAY!

THIS DOESN'T SEEM VERY SECRET.

BOY, AM I GLAD I RAN INTO YOU.

HA, I GET IT!

WHERE'D SHE GO?

I'VE GOT A *BAD* FEELING ABOUT THIS.

HURRY, ROCKS, THE GAME'S AFOOT!

RUNNING IS *NOT* A GAME! I *HATE* RUNNING!

YOU, WAITRESS, WHERE DID THEY GO?

NO ONE CAME OUT *THIS* WAY.

DON'T WORRY, THEY CAN'T OUTTRICK ME! I KNOW ALL THE ESCAPE TECHNIQUES.

WORRY? I NEVER WORRY WHEN THERE'S *FOOD*.

HEY GUYS, I'M REALLY SORRY ABOUT THIS, BUT YOU GUYS ARE WANTED AND I HAVE A *QUEST* THAT NEEDS FULFILLING.

WHAT? WHAT JUST HAPPENED?

I NEEDED TO CATCH YOU SO I COULD CLAIM THE *REWARD MONEY* TO FUND MY QUEST. SO I BUILT THIS THING. IT'S LIKE A MODIFIED CATAPULT.

YOU *BUILT* THIS? WHILE WE WERE IN THE RESTAURANT?

YEAH, SORRY ABOUT THAT. I DIDN'T MEAN TO KEEP YOU WAITING.

WAIT, YOU'RE BOTH *GIRLS?*

YOU *REALLY* BUILT ALL THIS?

SHE'S THE *PRINCESS*, ACTUALLY. WE'RE ON A QUEST.

AWW MAN, THIS IS NOT FAIR. WHAT ABOUT *MY* QUEST?

YOU HAVE A QUEST TOO?

YEAH, IT'S KIND OF A LONG STORY.

WELL, WE CAN'T LEAVE TILL THOSE BOUNTY HUNTERS DO, SO LET'S *HEAR* IT.

Princeless!

M Moriarty 2012

PIN-UP BY MERIDITH MORIARTY

NINETY DAYS. NINETY DAYS I'VE BEEN LOCKED IN THIS TOWER AND NO ONE HAS EVEN *TRIED* TO RESCUE ME.

POOR PRINCESS RAVEN, NOBODY COMES LOOKING FOR YOU. YOU'RE NOT EVEN A PROPER PRINCESS.

JUST CALL ME *PRINCESS LAME-O!* JUST STARING OUT YOUR...

WHOOOSH!

WHAT WAS THAT? WHO'S THERE?

NOBODY?

FIGURES. PROBABLY JUST A CLOUD. BACK TO BEING MISERABLE.

HELLO?

HELLO?

HI THERE!

Girls Who Fight Boys

STORY: JEREMY WHITLEY
ART: EMILY C. MARTIN
COLORS: SOOJIN PAEK
LETTERS: DAVE DWONCH

YOU LOOK LIKE YOU NEED TO BE RESCUED.

UMMM... YES PLEASE, IF YOU DON'T MIND.

AWESOME! LET ME GO PARK MY DRAGON AND I'LL BE RIGHT BACK.

SWEET! YOU SHOULD KNOW THAT THERE'S A KNIGHT DOWN THERE THAT WILL PROBABLY FIGHT YOU.

NO SWEAT! WE CAN TAKE CARE OF IT. I'M ADRIENNE ASHE, BY THE WAY.

I'M RAVEN XINGTAO. KICK HIS BUTT!

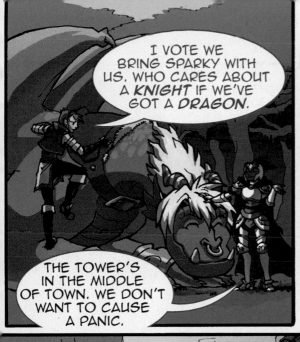

I VOTE WE BRING SPARKY WITH US. WHO CARES ABOUT A *KNIGHT* IF WE'VE GOT A *DRAGON*.

THE TOWER'S IN THE MIDDLE OF TOWN. WE DON'T WANT TO CAUSE A PANIC.

WE'RE SUPPOSED TO BE SAVING YOUR SISTERS. REMIND ME WHY ARE WE STOPPING HERE?

NO GIRL DESERVES TO BE LOCKED UP IN A TOWER, BEDELIA. I'VE BEEN THERE. IT STINKS.

SO...WE'RE JUST GONNA RESCUE EVERYBODY NOW?

WELL, I RESCUED YOU DIDN'T I?

THAT'S NOT QUITE HOW I REMEMBER IT GOING...

THIS MUST BE THE KNIGHT SHE WAS TALKING ABOUT.

HE DOESN'T LOOK TOO TOUGH.

NOW HERE COMES A BRAVE KNIGHT TO SHOW YOU ALL HOW IT'S DONE!

DO YOU MIND IF I RESCUE THIS PRINCESS?

BY ALL MEANS, SIR KNIGHT. PLEASE DO.

IF I CAN JUST TAKE THIS OFF...

I REALLY WISH WE HAD BROUGHT THE DRAGON.

G A S P!

BLASPHEMING WOMAN! COME HERE AND BE PUNISHED.

EXCUSE ME?

I SAID COME HERE!

THAT'S SIR ZACHARY THE PURE. HE IS THE GREATEST AND PUREST KNIGHT IN ALL THE LAND.

WHO'S THIS JOKER?

HMMM...

YOU KEEP TRYING TO GET THAT GRAPPLING HOOK UP THERE. I'M GOING TO TAKE CARE OF THIS DOOFUS.

BE CAREFUL.

I DON'T NEED TO BE CAREFUL. THIS GUY DOESN'T LOOK LIKE HE COULD OUT FIGHT A KITTEN.

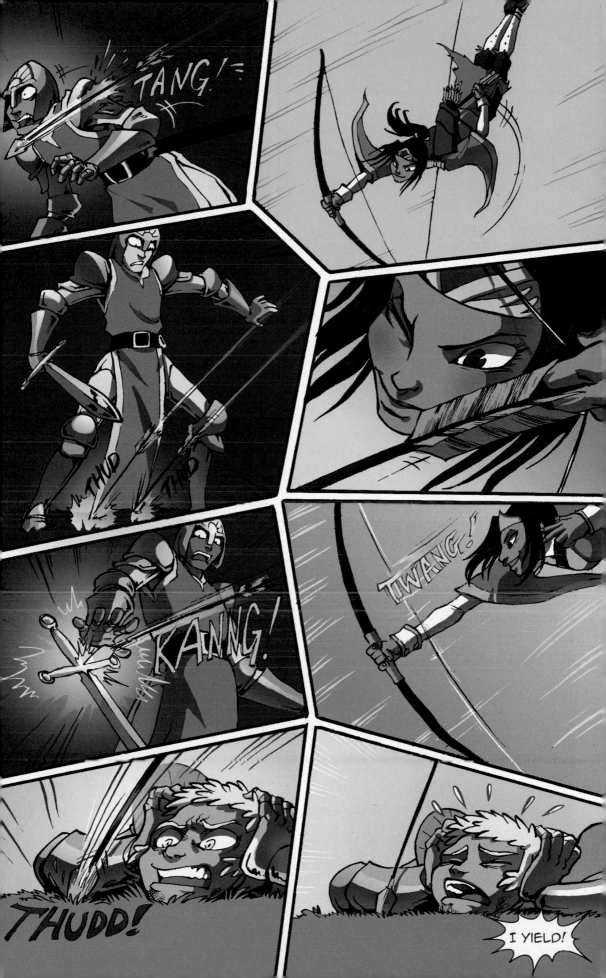

I SAID I YIELDED!

THIS HUMILIATION IS NOT VERY LADYLIKE OF YOU.

YEAH, WELL, WE'RE NOT VERY LADY-LIKE.

I NEVER SAID I WAS.

BURP!

HA HA HA HA HA HA HA HA HA HA

EXCUSE ME.

SO, WHERE DOES A PRINCESS LEARN TO USE A BOW LIKE THAT?

OH, WELL, I'M NOT EXACTLY A PRINCESS, THOUGH MY FATHER DOES CALL HIMSELF A KING.

HOW CAN YOU BE THE DAUGHTER OF A KING AND NOT A PRINCESS?

WELL, MY FATHER IS THE PIRATE KING. AND BOY WILL HE BE MAD WHEN HE HEARS YOU GUYS LET ME OUT.

GULP!

If you don't know someone with autism today you will.

1 in 88 Children are Diagnosed with an Autism Spectrum Disorder

Autism Speaks
is leading the way
into researching
the causes of autism
and how to better
treat and diagnose it.
We need your help.

Donate, volunteer or join
a Walk team and
let your voice be heard.

AUTISM SPEAKS™
It's time to listen.

www.AutismSpeaks.org